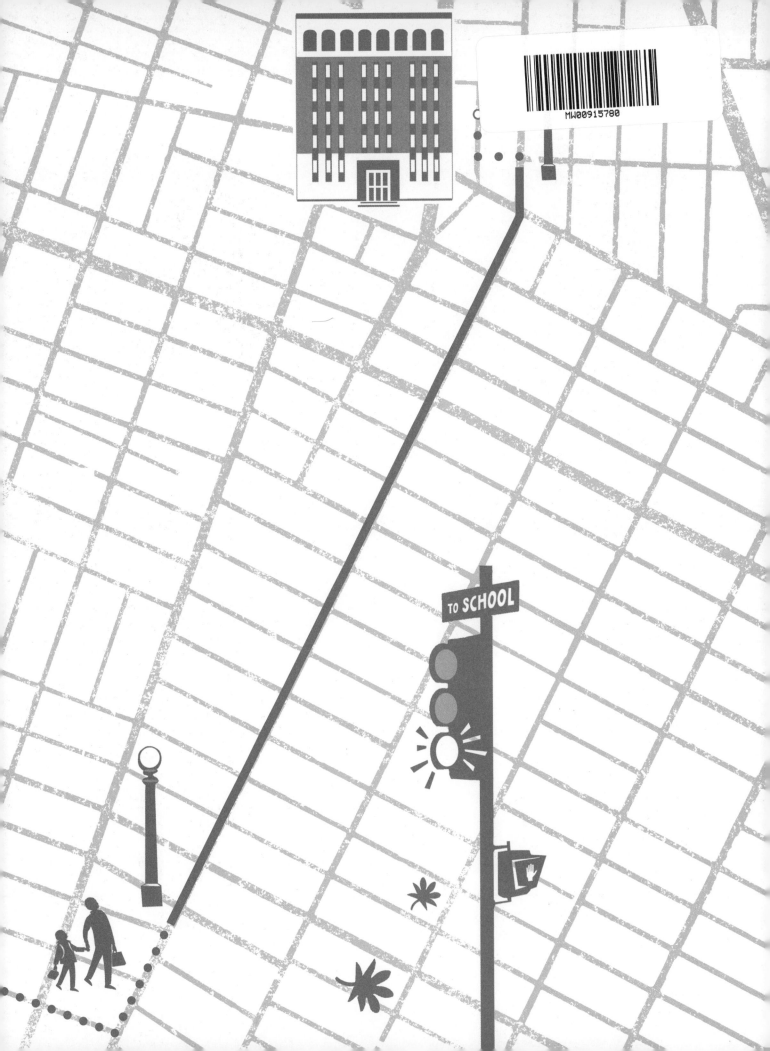

TO SCHOOL

Out
the door

Christy Hale

NEAL PORTER BOOKS

HOLIDAY HOUSE / NEW YORK

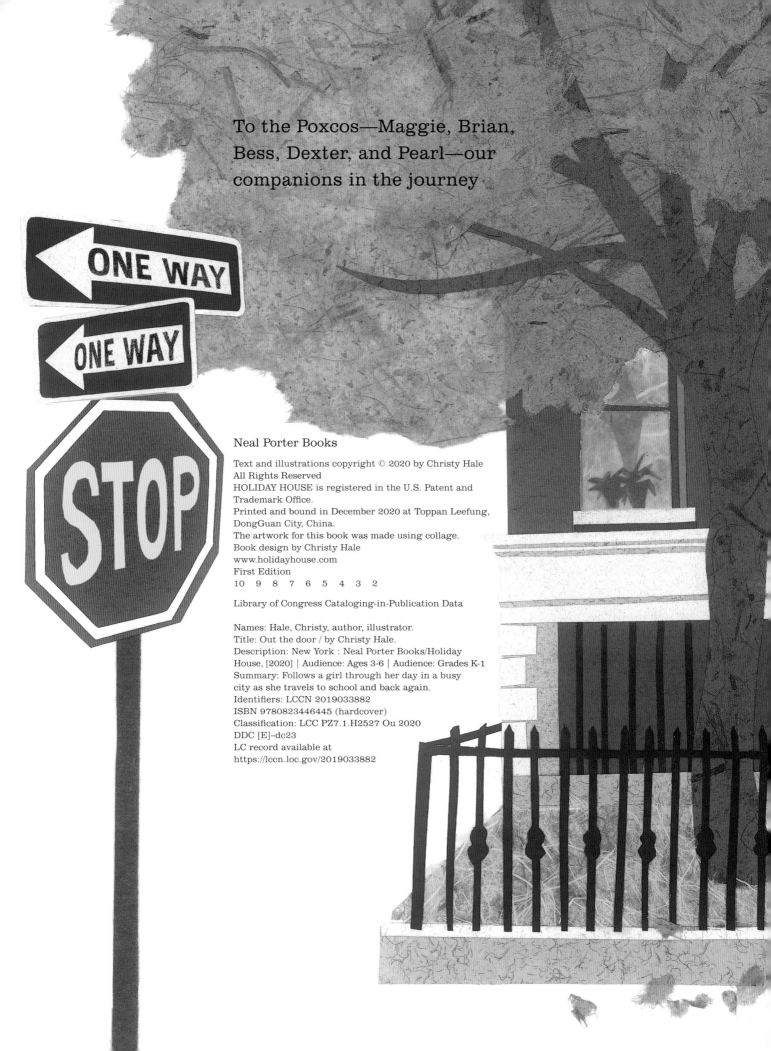

To the Poxcos—Maggie, Brian,
Bess, Dexter, and Pearl—our
companions in the journey

Neal Porter Books

Text and illustrations copyright © 2020 by Christy Hale
All Rights Reserved
HOLIDAY HOUSE is registered in the U.S. Patent and
Trademark Office.
Printed and bound in December 2020 at Toppan Leefung,
DongGuan City, China.
The artwork for this book was made using collage.
Book design by Christy Hale
www.holidayhouse.com
First Edition
10 9 8 7 6 5 4 3 2

Library of Congress Cataloging-in-Publication Data

Names: Hale, Christy, author, illustrator.
Title: Out the door / by Christy Hale.
Description: New York : Neal Porter Books/Holiday
House, [2020] | Audience: Ages 3-6 | Audience: Grades K-1
Summary: Follows a girl through her day in a busy
city as she travels to school and back again.
Identifiers: LCCN 2019033882
ISBN 9780823446445 (hardcover)
Classification: LCC PZ7.1.H2527 Ou 2020
DDC [E]–dc23
LC record available at
https://lccn.loc.gov/2019033882

down the stoop

past the neighbors **along** the block

up to the light

across the street

outside
the station

at the booth

beyond the turnstile

below the ground

amid the crowd

behind the line

aboard the train **on** a seat

through a tunnel **in** the dark

to my stop

F JAMAICA-179 ST

← F A C →

Jay St-MetroTech S

up the stairs

into daylight

around
the corner

inside my school

among my friends

until it's time

for home

and then . . .

out the door

down the steps

past my friends

below the ground

amid the crowd **behind** the line

aboard the train **on** a seat

to my stop

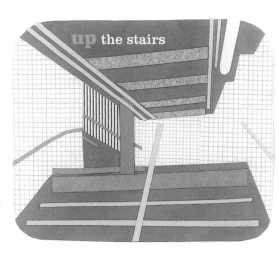

up the stairs

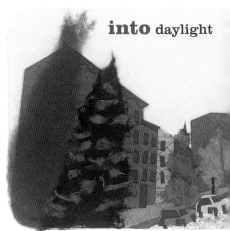

into daylight

among family

until it's time

along the street

outside the station

beyond the turnstile

through a tunnel **in** the dark

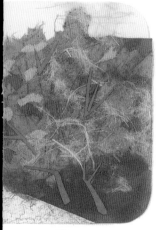

around the corner

inside my house

for bed

and then . . .

out the door.